Mug Shots

by **Anne Dineen**

illustrated by **Rae Dale**

The Characters

Stephen

Scully and his Gang

The Setting

CONTENTS

CHAPTER 1

The Four Skulls

Terror had a new name for the Year 3s.
That name was 'The Four Skulls'.

The Four Skulls were four tough Year 6s.
They had taken over the path between
the tuck shop and the Year 3s' classroom.

It wasn't a big area, but it was big enough to be out of sight of the teachers. As the Year 3s walked by, the gang would select a victim.

The latest victim was Tim. They demanded his lunch money, and the contents of his backpack were dumped onto the ground.

As Tim tried to pick up his stuff, two
of The Skulls shoved him hard. So hard,
that Tim fell over and grazed his knees.

By the time Tim had picked up all his things, the bell had gone. He barely made it into class on time.

Tim's brand-new school things were scratched and dirty. He was hurt but everyone was too afraid to tell. All of them were shaken and upset. In fact, nothing was said by anyone.

The whole class just looked at Tim. Earlier victims knew how he felt. The rest didn't want to know, but they knew they would, sooner or later. It was just a matter of time. The bullies didn't pounce every day — just most days.

CHAPTER 2

Stephen's Turn

Eventually it was Stephen's turn. He almost made it to the classroom steps, but they grabbed him, pack and all, and dragged him down the side.

"OK dork, hand over your money," Scully demanded.

"I don't have any lunch money. Mum makes my lunch," said Stephen as he squirmed, trying to get away.

"He doesn't have any lunch money. Mummy makes it," Scully said with a whine.

"Poor little baby! Well let's see what you've got for lunch, DORK!"

They dumped Stephen's things all over the grass and walked on a few of his books.

Then they raided his lunch box.

"Jam sandwiches? You call that lunch? That's pitiful!" Scully scowled as he threw Stephen's lunch over the fence.

"But what's this? £5 and a note —
Art supplies money .... That'll do fine!"

"Give that back! I have to give that
to Miss Thompson this morning,"
Stephen pleaded.

"Who's going to make us, dork? Get real."

They gave him an extra shove and ran off to class as the bell rang.

And so it was that Stephen turned up a little late for class with a bloody knee, a bloody elbow, a torn shirt and no art supplies money.

Miss Thompson was taking the register and was almost up to Stephen when he walked in. She gave him a hard look but didn't say anything. She marked him present and said, "Stephen, do you have your art supplies money today?"

Stephen flushed, swallowed hard and said, "I had it this morning, but ummm ..."

The class fell silent. They knew what had happened. Would Stephen tell her?

After a long silence, Miss Thompson said, "Stephen?"

"Umm, I lost it. I'm sorry, Miss Thompson."

And twenty-five kids breathed again.

"Oh Stephen, that's not like you. I'm very disappointed."

Stephen was crushed. He thought Miss Thompson was the greatest thing since his mum. She was pretty and nice and all the kids loved her. Now she was disappointed in him and it wasn't even his fault!

He also had to figure out what he was going to tell his parents about the £5. Telling them the truth about the bullies wasn't an option. Parents just didn't understand about bullies, especially The Four Skulls. You either did what they said or they'd be after you. Stephen didn't want to spend every day looking over his shoulder.

CHAPTER 3

A Clever Idea

When Stephen got home, his mum was at the computer working on a poster for his dad's birthday. It said, "WANTED" (with a photo of his dad underneath) "for ...".

She had stopped there as she tried to think of the final phrase.

"How shall I finish it, Stephen?" she asked. "For the best 40th birthday party ever? Or ... what do you think?"

"I don't know, Mum," Stephen answered.

But as he watched her, an idea began to form. He was good with computers, and his mum's program was easy to use.

If he could only get some proof —
a photo or something — he could make
a poster of the bullies. He could put it
up where the teachers could see it.
Then The Four Skulls wouldn't know who
had grassed them up.

Stephen thought about it over the next few days. He couldn't figure out how he could get close enough to take a photo. If he was seen, he'd be turned into playground pizza.

Three weeks had gone by, and the bullies were really getting into it. They sat across the path, blocking it, making the kids walk around them. Every Year 3 kid was scared, not knowing whether today was going to be their day.

One morning, Stephen was called up onto the balcony by Miss Thompson.

"Stephen, would you like to help me water these plants for a week? We're going to grow them as a class project."

"Yes, Miss Thompson. What would you like me to do?"

"Good," Stephen thought. "She's not mad at me anymore."

"Water them every morning this week. Give them extra water on Friday so that there is water in their saucers."

As Stephen watered the plants, he leant
over the flower stand and looked down.
He couldn't believe it! The bullies' arena
was just below. He could take a photo
from up here!

"Yes!" he thought, as he punched the air.
"I'll bring my camera tomorrow!"

Thursday was his mum's day in town, so she drove him to school. Stephen got to school early. He ran up to the balcony, watered the plants and waited. He waited for ages. Soon it was time to go in and nothing had happened.

For two more days Stephen got to school early, but nothing happened. There was no real bully action. Scully and the gang had scared some girls by walking up quickly behind them, but nothing else. Stephen was beginning to think that The Four Skulls had found another place.

CHAPTER 4

The Proof

Then on Tuesday they pounced, and Stephen was waiting with his camera.

Their victim was Henry. He was running late and not paying attention. He ran right into the roadblock the gang of four had formed.

Stephen zoomed in and got a clear shot. The Four Skulls did the usual as Stephen snapped away.

Stephen could hardly wait to take his film to the shop on his way home. He had taken some photos over the Christmas holidays anyway, so he had an excuse for wanting them.

Now all he had to do was pick them up.

Stephen's dad always went shopping on Thursday nights, so Stephen offered to go with him and help.

As they walked into the shopping centre,
Stephen raced off to get the photos.
He flipped through the others. Then, there
they were, The Four Skulls in action, all
with their very own 'mug shots'. He quickly
hid them in his pocket.

"Are they the holiday photos?" asked his dad. "Are there any good ones, Stephen?"

"Yeah, I've got some interesting ones, I think. I'll show them to you at home," Stephen said.

Later, as his parents cooked dinner, Stephen worked on the computer. He placed the photos onto the scanner. It only took a couple of minutes and then he was ready.

Using his mum's WANTED poster, Stephen removed his dad's photo from the frame. He replaced it with four action shots. With a bit of cropping and enlarging he had it.

Next, he looked up the word he was searching for. Finally, there it was: '**extortion**' — to obtain money by force, torture or threat.

"Perfect," he said.

The poster now read: WANTED FOR
BULLYING AND EXTORTION. At the
bottom he added 'Watch from the
balcony, 8:30–9:00am for more proof'.

He printed out two copies of his poster.

CHAPTER 5

Justice

On Monday morning, Stephen got to school at 8:00am. He slipped one poster under the door of the Head's office and stuck the other one on the staffroom door.

43

"It's showtime!" said Stephen, and he crossed his fingers and waited.

The first one to arrive was Miss Thompson.
She pulled the poster off the staffroom
door.

About 10 minutes later, she was joined by Mr Clark, the Head.

"I see you have one of these too."

"Yes. It was on the door when I opened up this morning. What do you think?"

"I think we should watch and see what happens," Mr Clark replied.

At about 8:50am the bullies struck, in front of a very interested audience.

The teachers were surprised, and the Head was furious.

The whole school was called to a special assembly after lunch.

"You have all been called here to identify some Year 6s. They are well known to many of you," the Head began.

He called out the names of the four bullies. They slowly walked up to the front of the hall.

"Take a good look at these four. They are bullies. They pick on younger, smaller children and take what does not belong to them. They are nothing to be afraid of. This is their last day as bullies."

Mr Clark paused and turned to look directly at the four boys. "You will be severely dealt with. I will not tolerate bullying in any form at this school. Is that clear? IS THAT CLEAR?"

As Mr Clark repeated his last line, he turned and looked out at the sea of faces.

"Yes, Sir," the stunned assembly murmured. As they went back to class there was much whispering and lots of questions. "What will happen to Scully?" "How did the teachers find out?" "Did someone grass them up?"

The Year 3s were happy that they didn't have to be scared anymore. Stephen smiled but kept quiet.

CHAPTER  6

Stephen's Own Mug Shot

Weeks went by and one day, Stephen's mum found a disk with no label. She pushed it into the computer and up came the file *Mug Shots*. As she saw the poster open up, she started to laugh. The parents had all heard of the famous poster which had stopped the bullies, but no one knew where it had come from.

She added a line to the bottom.

"To Stephen for outstanding work on your Mug Shots project." Then she printed it out, put it in a frame and placed it on the kitchen table.

Stephen came home, called out 'hello', raided the fridge and stopped cold as he went to sit down at the kitchen table. There was his poster in a frame.

"That was an interesting project, Stephen. Did you get a good mark for it?" his mother asked.

"Mum, I can explain ..."

"I'm sure you can, Honey. I just want you to know how proud I am of you." She stopped and smiled. "However, if you ever use my colour printer without permission again, you'll have your own mug shot! Understood?"

GLOSSARY

crushed
let down

demanded
asked with force

eventually
finally

grazed
took the skin off

pitiful
sad, worthless

pleaded
begged

pounce
to grab suddenly

raided
attacked

severely
very strictly

squirmed
wriggled

tolerate
put up with

victim
someone who is hurt
or picked on

Anne Dineen

What is your favourite thing?

My camera.

What do you like about yourself?

I am very well organised and have a well developed sense of humour.

Why did the cow jump over the moon?

She really wanted to moove it!

What is your best midnight snack?

Biscuits and champagne.

Rae Dale

What is your favourite thing?

Books.

What do you like about yourself?

A sense of the ridiculous.

Why did the cow jump over the moon?

Why not?

What is your best midnight snack?

A delicious autobiography.